Alice &
Anatole

For Katherine Halligan and Genevieve Webster,
my dream team

SIMON AND SCHUSTER

First published in Great Britain in 2007 by Simon & Schuster UK Ltd

Africa House, 64–78 Kingsway, London WC2B 6AH

A CBS COMPANY

This paperback edition first published 2007

Text and illustrations copyright © 2007 Sam Childs

The right of Sam Childs to be identified as the author
and illustrator of this work has been asserted by her in accordance
with the Copyright, Designs and Patents Act, 1988

Book designed by Genevieve Webster
The text for this book is set in Monotype Bell
The illustrations are rendered in watercolour

A CIP catalogue record for this book is available from
the British Library upon request

ISBN 1 416 90484 0

EAN 9781416904847

Printed in China

1 3 5 7 9 10 8 6 4 2

Alice & Anatole

Sam Childs

SIMON AND SCHUSTER
London New York Sydney

Alice loved dancing, reading
and doing handstands.

She especially loved her new red shoes.

But even though she had a beautiful bedroom full of books
and toys, she had no friends to share them with.
Alice was lonely.

She just couldn't figure out How to Make Friends.
The other children made it look so easy.
But she couldn't simply go up to someone and just *ask*
them to be her friend. What if they laughed at her?
It was much too difficult and scary.

At night, Alice dreamt of meeting wonderful new friends,
but when she woke up she always felt shy all over again.
One morning, she looked over the side of her bed
to say hello to her shoes as usual . . . But they were gone!

Then, out from under the bed, a pink nose appeared,
pushing gently at the valance.
"A pet rabbit?" she whispered, hopefully.
The nose grew and grew and GREW, until . . .

"What *are* you?" gasped Alice.
"I'm Anatole," it said. "I'm an anteater. I eat ants."
"That is revolting," giggled Alice. "Not an attractive habit at all."

Then she noticed his feet.
"Oh!" she shrieked. "Give them back, RIGHT NOW!"
But Anatole was feeling playful.

Reluctantly, Anatole gave Alice
back her shoes.
"Sorry," he snuffled. "Can we still be friends?"
"We'll see," said Alice.

And, sure enough, by breakfast time they were great mates.

At the library, things got a bit out of hand.
But Alice met a lovely girl with pink ribbons.

At the park, things got even wilder.
Alice met a funny boy with a magic cape.
Alice invited her new friends home to play.
She was terribly excited.

Alice and her new friends had a lovely time playing.
But Anatole felt left out. Until . . .

. . . with one great swoosh of his tail,
everyone suddenly remembered him again.

"Anatole!" said Alice. "Leave me alone!
You've spoilt our game, you have bad manners and
a yucky tongue and I DON'T want to be your friend!
I've got better friends now."

"Don't care," said Anatole.
But he did, so he slid away and hid.

That night, Alice felt lonelier than ever.
Life without Anatole just wasn't the same.

The next morning, Alice looked under the bed.
Anatole wasn't there.

"Maybe my shoes will cheer me up," Alice thought.
So she put them on, and went to admire herself in the mirror.

From his hiding place, Anatole watched as she struggled
to see her shoes in the mirror. But Alice was too small, and the
mirror was too high up on the wall.

Anatole watched as Alice stood up on the edge of the toilet seat.
He watched as she balanced, and stretched, and wobbled . . .

KERSPLASH! Anatole watched as Alice's left shoe
went – PLOP! – right down into the toilet.

Alice was distraught.
"My beautiful shoe!" she wailed. And she sat down on the
floor and sobbed her heart out.
Alice did not see Anatole, as he crept up to the toilet.

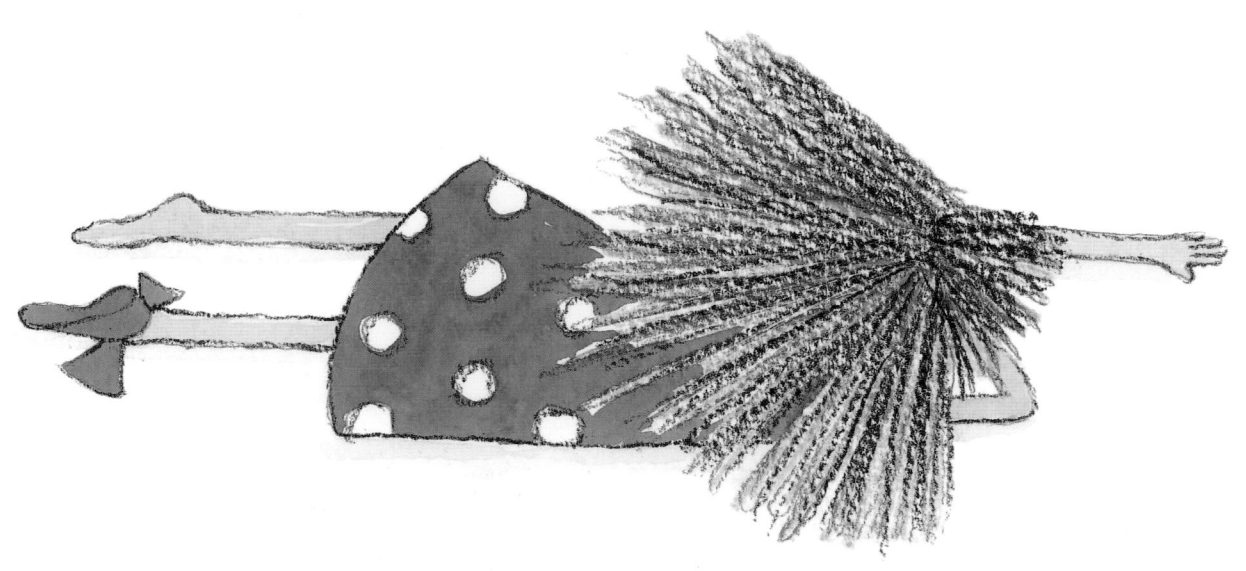

She didn't see him stretching his little head as far as he could.
She didn't see him reaching for the edge,
sticking his long nose down inside...
and snatching up her shoe!

"Oh, Anatole!" squeaked Alice. "My shoe!
You're the best!"

And she gave him an enormous thank-you hug.

That afternoon, at the park, Alice and Anatole played
all their favourite games, and had a marvellous time
with their new friends.

"You're not revolting, Anatole," said Alice. "You're lovely."
And they made their way back home.

Later that evening, when Alice and Anatole were both
clean and dry, they snuggled down together in a big chair
and Alice read a story to Anatole.
"Best friends?" he whispered.

"Forever!" said Alice.